Come

There's a

For Victoria Wells Arms,
with three cheers,
and to Jill Davis, who got
this party started
—J.M.

For my wonderful parents
and family, who always
gave me the opportunity
to play!
—S.T.

Hippo Park

An imprint of Astra Books for Young Readers, a division of Astra Publishing House
astrapublishinghouse.com
Printed in China

ISBN: 978-1-6626-4000-1 (hc)
ISBN: 978-1-6626-4001-8 (eBook)
Library of Congress Control Number: 2021922643

First edition

10 9 8 7 6 5 4 3 2 1

Design by Dana Fritts and Amelia Mack
The text is set in Arquitecta
The titles are set in KansasNew and Goodlife
The illustrations are done in still life and photography

on in!

Party in this Book!

Written by
Jamie Michalak

Illustrated by
Sabine Timm

Hippo Park

What?!
There's a **party** in this book?
Come on, Lemon!
Let's go look.

Knock,
Knock!

Is this is a **mouse** party?

A **pants, sock,** and **house** party?

No! This is a game where we can't touch the floor.

Lemon, keep looking.
Try the next door.

Knock, Knock!

Is the **party** in here?

Nope!

Just **cats** wearing **boots.**

No party here either!

Just **fruits** dressed in **suits!**

So where is the party?
Has it begun?

Rat-a-tat-tat

Lemon, keep looking. This book is not done.

Is this a **log** party?
A **globe, brush,**
and **dog** party?

No! These are five friends enjoying the sea.

But no party here.
Where could it be?

These are some pigeons.

Their names are all . . .

Fred!

And this is a kitchen

for **cake** and for **bread.**

Is there really a party?
Now Lemon's back home.

Does the book end right here,
with her sad and alone?

Wait! An idea! Here's what to do—

Let's make our own party.
You can help, too!

and shout,

Come on in!

Finally! The party's about to begin!

This is a mouse and a pants,
sock, and house party.
This is a dog and a brush,
globe, and frog party.

A bread and a Fred party,
a stand on your head party,
a twist and a shout and
a **no one left out** party!

This is a big and a small,
have a ball party.

Hooray for new friends at the
come one and all party!

Come on in!